Old MacDonald Had an Apartment House

written by **Judi Barrett**

illustrated by **Ron Barrett**

Atheneum Books for Young Readers

Atheneum Books for Young Readers
An imprint of Simon & Schuster Children's Publishing Division
1230 Avenue of the Americas
New York, New York 10020
The text of this book is set in Caslon 540BT.
Printed in Hong Kong by South China Printing Co. (1988) Ltd.
First Atheneum Books for Young Readers Edition, 1969.
Revised Format Edition, 1998.
10 9 8 7 6 5 4 3 2 1
Library of Congress Catalog-in-Publication Data
Barrett, Judi.
Old MacDonald had an apartment house / written by Judith Barrett and
illustrated by Ron Barrett.—2nd ed.
p. cm.
Summary: Mr. MacDonald, an apartment super, turns his building into a
four-story farm with hot and cold running sweet potato vines, ceiling carrots,
carpets of cabbages, and other farm produce and animals, prompting
all the tenants to move out.
ISBN 0-689-81757-6
[1. Apartment houses—Fiction. 2. Farms—Fiction. 3. Humorous stories.]
I. Barrett, Ron, ill. II. Title.
PZ7.B275201   1998
[E]—dc21
97-17349

Dedicated to all children everywhere.
(Even those who hate vegetables.)

Old MacDonald lived in a big apartment house with his wife
and their dog. He didn't own the building. Fat Mr. Wrental did. Old
MacDonald was its Super.

He polished the brass doorknobs when they got smudgy, mopped up the hallways when they got dirty, and sent up steam when it got cold.

Old MacDonald's apartment was on the bottom floor and was very dark.

The windows were covered by a thick bushy hedge that grew in the front yard.

Without sunlight, his wife's tomato plant grew pale and droopy.

So, Old MacDonald decided to cut down the hedge in front of the windows.

With all the sunlight that came in, the plant straightened up, grew a few leaves, and even grew a few tomatoes.

But the spot where the hedge had been looked very empty, so
Old MacDonald's wife suggested that they fill it with her tomato plant. And
they did.

It grew lots of new leaves, many more tomatoes, and much much taller.

"Why not get rid of the rest of the hedge," Old MacDonald said. "Then instead, I could plant vegetables in the yard. They're better looking than the hedge and much better tasting, too." So he cut the whole hedge down to the ground and in its place he planted rows of corn and melons and beans and radishes. The fountain became a self-watering pea patch.

The front yard had become a small farm and the tenants were amazed.

One of the tenants, Mrs. Katz, really didn't need four rooms anymore.
Her children were grown up. So, she moved out.

It occurred to Old MacDonald then that an empty apartment would be a good place to grow lots more vegetables. He quickly moved in some soil and proceeded to redecorate in Late Vegetarian style. He laid down a carpet of carrots and cabbages, put some sweet potatoes where the couch had been, and stuffed the closet with mushrooms.

Some days later, Mrs. Katz's downstairs neighbor, Mr. Hopkins, turned on a faucet and got hot and cold running sweet potato vines. Above his head he could see carrots popping through the ceiling. He became furious. "Either that garden up there goes or I go," he screamed at Old MacDonald.

But Old MacDonald really didn't care. He had begun to feel that in some ways vegetables made better tenants than people. Carrots didn't smudge brass doorknobs. Cucumbers didn't leave muddy footprints in the halls. And potatoes didn't bang on the radiators for more steam.

Angry Mr. Hopkins moved out.

A variety of vegetables, a field of clover, and a cow moved in.

No one knew what Old MacDonald was doing, but you can't
keep a cow a secret for very long.

More and more people moved out, very disgusted with what was happening.

So, more vegetables, fruit trees, cows, and chickens took their place.

Finally every tenant in the building had moved out. The apartment house became a four-story farm.

Then one day Fat Mr. Wrental, the owner, stopped by to check on the house and collect the rent money, as he did every few months. When he saw that his tenants had been replaced by vegetables, fruit trees, cows, and chickens, he got upset. Very upset.

"Look here Old MacDonald, what have you done?"
he shouted. "Where are the families? All that's here now
are bushels of fruits and vegetables, herds of cows,
and flocks of chickens. And they can't pay me rent."

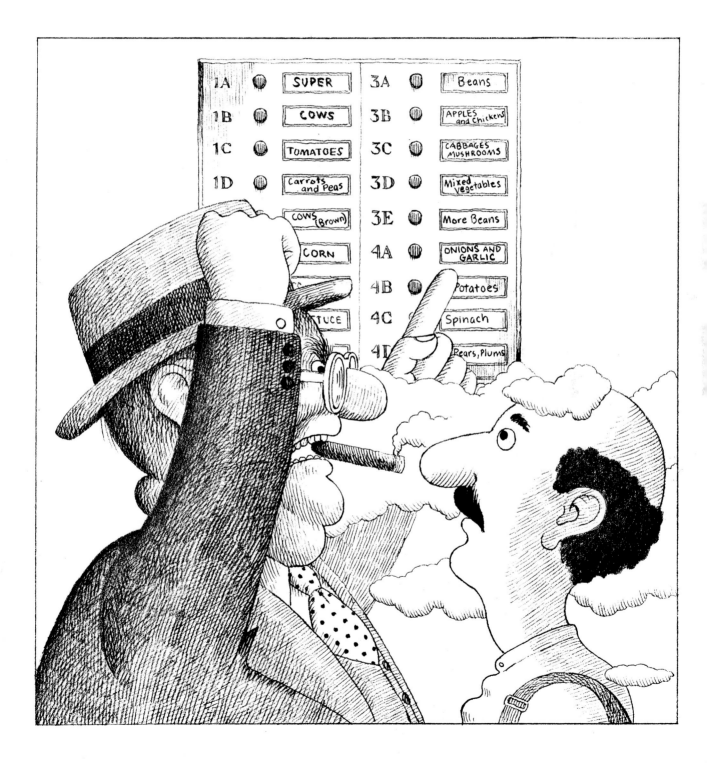

Old MacDonald and his wife were very sad. They knew they would have to leave. Fat Mr. Wrental told them so. In fact, he was going to have the whole farm thrown out into the street.

Old MacDonald told his wife not to cry near her tomato plant because the salt water wouldn't be good for it.

Besides, it set a bad example for the cows.

Fat Mr. Wrental paced back and forth quickly in front of the house. He was very upset and not really sure that he liked the idea of throwing the farm out into the street. Old MacDonald had been such a good Super. Now not only was he without tenants, but he'd be without a Super, too.

"Who ever heard of a farm in the middle of the city? That's absurd," he muttered. "Or is it? Maybe a farm could pay me rent after all."

MELON

The next morning Old Mac-
Donald and his wife stepped outside
the house carrying their suitcases,
and in the middle of the front walk
Fat Mr. Wrental was building
a store. There was a big sign that
read 'Wrental and MacDonald's
Fruits and Vegetables—Fresh Milk
and Eggs Hourly.'

Fat Mr. Wrental waved at Old MacDonald and shouted, "Where are you going, partner? You grow the stuff and I'll sell it. Vegetables will pay me rent after all."

On opening day the store was jammed. Fat Mr. Wrental made a very long speech in which he asked everyone to come in very often and to buy as much as they could.

He asked Old MacDonald to say a few words, and he did. He said,

"People, I am happy to have such fine vegetables as tenants. I hope you agree that good vegetables make good neighbors."

The people applauded and then began to buy as much as they could. They came back day after day.

Both the store and the farm thrived throughout the summer and fall.

And even in winter, when the earth outside was frozen and covered

with snow, things were still growing on the steam-heated farm.

Judi Barrett grew up in an apartment house in Brooklyn similar to the one in this book and now lives in a smaller version of one, a brownstone.

She has written many award-winning books for young readers, including the classic *Cloudy with a Chance of Meatballs* and its recent, much-awaited sequel, *Pickles to Pittsburgh*.

When not writing for young readers she can be found teaching young artists at a private school in her neighborhood.

She has always had a special place in her heart for cows and chickens, but not in her apartment. And the only vegetables she has indoors are the ones in her refrigerator.

Ron Barrett is the illustrator of *Benjamin's 365 Birthdays*, *Animals should definitely <u>not</u> wear clothing*, *Cloudy with a Chance of Meatballs*, and *Pickles to Pittsburgh*, all written by Judi Barrett.

Ron Barrett's illustrations appear in a great variety of places, from The Hall of Early Mammals at New York City's American Museum of Natural History to ads for fast food. He's also the creator of the well-mannered comic strip *Politenessman*.

The illustrations for this book were honored by an exhibit in an apartment house in Paris where King Louis XIV had lived, known as the Louvre.